Ghost Striker at the Football Club

IAN WHYBROW

ILLUSTRATED BY MARK BEECH

Hodder
Children's
Books

For Dave

Buckinghamshire County Council	
15 170 693 6	
Askews & Holts	Nov-2013
JF	£4.99

Text copyright © 2013 Ian Whybrow
Illustrations copyright © 2013 Mark Beech
First published in Great Britain in 2013
by Hodder Children's Books

The rights of Ian Whybrow and Mark Beech to be identified as the Author and
Illustrator of the Work have been asserted by them in accordance with the
Copyright, Designs and Patents Act 1988.

1

A Catalogue record for this book is available from the British Library

ISBN 978 1 444 91572 3

Printed and bound by CPI Group (UK) Ltd, Croydon, CR0 4YY

The paper and board used in this paperback by
Hodder Children's Books are natural recyclable products made from
wood grown in sustainable forests. The manufacturing processes conform
to the environmental regulations of the country of origin.

Hodder Children's Books
A division of Hachette Children's Books
338 Euston Road, London NW1 3BH
An Hachette UK company
www.hachette.co.uk

The Haunted Wood

Hi, I'm Jake Treasure. I've got my dog and I've got my football. We're off for a bit of a kick-about on the common. Do you fancy joining us? Come on, then. And while we're having a run round, I'll tell you how my dad brought Spellthorpe United back from the dead – with a bit of help from me and a ghost or two.

It all started one Saturday about a year ago on the same common with the same big old dog called Lolly. My dad Neville was with us.

He was in a mood.

Loll kept bouncing up to him with my old football in her mouth but he ignored her. He just pushed on with his hands in his pockets, clucking his tongue at the golfers and muttering, "Hopeless! I'd like to get out there and show 'em how to play properly."

"Why don't you?" I asked. "You're always saying you'll show me how to play, but you never get round to it."

"Yeah, well. Too busy. I've got Mr Robinson after me to finish a report for work."

That Mr Robinson! He made

Dad's life a misery. I tried to cheer him up. "Boot the ball for Loll, Dad!" I called. "She's dying to have a run after it."

"You kick it," he answered. "Get off, Lolly! I haven't got the energy."

Dad used to love a kick-about. He could do anything with a ball, especially a football. "It's not fair,

making you work at the weekend,"
I said. "Why don't you pack that job
in and get another one?"

"Don't be so stupid," he said, but
I could tell he agreed with me
really. We trudged on.

Just across the lane there was
this fenced-off, scruffy bit of
woodland. Partly to change the
subject, I asked, "Why don't we

have a quick wander through those trees before we go back?"

Dad just pointed to an old sign that read,

Private Property. Danger! KEEP OUT!

"What's dangerous about it?" I wanted to know.

"Spellthorpe F.C. stadium," Dad said.

"What d'you mean?"

"Somewhere in the middle of all those trees there's a football ground they closed about eighty years ago. They say it was quite a

big stadium, but the whole thing must be a ruin now."

"I wish we had a football ground now," I said. "Why did they close it?"

"Search me," said Dad. "Come on. I've got to get back." He turned towards home.

"Oh, Dad," I whined. "Can't we just nip into the wood and have a sneaky peek around?"

"No way," he said. "No time and not interested. Anyway, we'll have spooks after us. I've heard the place is haunted."

A Start for Spellthorpe Youth F.C.

I knew Dad didn't believe in ghosts,
so I thought he was just making one
up to try to put me off exploring
the wood. Still, I kept on firing
questions at him.

"Blimey, you're worse than
Lolly!" he groaned, meaning that
once I got my teeth into something,
I wouldn't let go.

But I kept at him, and finally
Dad remembered that the club had

been owned by some mad bloke called Wicks who'd made a fortune as a shipwreck-hunter and then died suddenly.

That might have been the end of it, but a couple of days later Dad called me over to his laptop. "Here," he said. "I've found something that might interest you."

I peered at the screen. It was an old issue of *The Spellthorpe Gazette*,

dated May 9, 1921, with a story about the death of Ernie (Sailor) Wicks.

"I thought you weren't interested, Dad."

"Yeah, well," he said, giving me a friendly smack round the head. "I just thought I might check him out."

I ran my eye over the page of old-fashioned print and there it was.

Mr Ernie (Sailor) Wicks, owner and player-manager of Spellthorpe F.C., a fine centre forward capable of shooting with both feet from anywhere on the pitch. He also earned himself a reputation as a man with an excellent nose for sunken treasure.

"You were right about the treasure-hunting, Dad," I said.

Mr Wicks made a fortune as captain of a specially built ship he named Spellthorpe Striker. He had at least three very lucky strikes, finding gold on wrecks he explored.

While he was away during the 1921 football season, Spellthorpe F.C. had a run of bad luck. Results went from bad to worse, good players started leaving and the crowds dwindled rapidly. The chairman was arrested for stealing the club funds, and less than a month later, the Spellthorpe Striker disappeared in thick fog off the Scilly Isles. It is presumed to have hit rocks and sunk without trace. There were no survivors.

"What does this mean?" I asked Dad, pointing out the words on the screen, "The club went into liquidation."

"It means that the club hit the rocks and went down with the ship," said Dad with a sigh. "Rotten shame, eh?"

I agreed. "We could do with someone starting up a football team  around here," I added. "It would be great if they had one for kids my age." "Yeah, well, who's going to take that on?" Dad said gloomily.

It came to me in a flash. "Why not *you*?" I demanded. "You like football. You're good at it. Go on, Dad! We could call ourselves Spellthorpe Youth."

Dad looked shocked. "Me?" he said. "You must be joking.

Mr Robinson says I couldn't manage my way out of a paper bag."

I could tell, though, that he'd taken the bait about running a team. "So where would we play?" he asked me.

"We could play on the common to start with," I said, jumping up and getting excited. "Never mind about a proper pitch."

So that was how our team got started. I called up Robbie, Neil, Simon, Nickie, Cameron and Weeksie – and the following Sunday morning they all turned up to play, along with Cameron's dad Mr Aldridge.

"So what's happening, Mr Treasure?" said Mr Aldridge, holding

out a hand the size of a shovel. He drove a JCB and was built like a weight-lifter.

"Just a kick-about," said Dad. "D'you want to pick four lads?"

So Mr Aldridge picked Robbie, Neil, Simon and Weeksie and we played five against four with me, Cameron and Nickie on Dad's side. Robbie and Nickie played as rush-goalies. It turned out that neither Robbie nor Nickie had much idea how to trap the ball or pass or even give the ball a good whack, but they were keen as mustard and never stopped running.

Dad was easily the best player on the field. He was good at drawing the opposition and sending me and Cam into positions where we had a chance to score.

That game was a good laugh but it didn't last very long, mainly because the dads soon got puffed out. Our side won but not by much, and everyone was keen to have another go the following Sunday.

"Weeksie," panted Dad. "How do you fancy trying out for

goalkeeper?" Weeksie blushed and said he'd give it a go. "What say we meet up midweek for a training session?" Dad continued.

"Great idea, Skip," puffed Mr Aldridge with a wink. "Me and Cameron are up for that, aren't we, Cam?"

"Not 'arf!" said Cam, with a grin and all the rest of us kids let out a chorus like an echo: "NOT 'ARF!"

Some Serious Training

Dad took our training seriously from the start. Next time we met, all us lads got training bibs. We also had marker-cones, some to mark out the pitch and the rest to lay in a line for dribbling practice.

We didn't just play a game; we started off with some warm-up exercises, a long jog round the common, then did some sprints and press-ups and some heading and passing. Only after all that would he let us get got stuck into a match.

News got round about what we were up to and it wasn't long before other lads wanted to join in. Suddenly there were fourteen of us! More lads meant more dads putting in money. Gradually we got together more footballs, a pair of pretty smart second-hand goals and other stuff like speed hurdles and passing arcs. In training, you weren't allowed to score unless you threaded the ball through a passing

arc on the way. If you were going at speed, that took a bit of doing.

One morning, at breakfast, Dad came out with something that made me and Mum sit up. "I've decided we're going to have to join the local league if we want to play proper matches," he said, "so I'm going on a coaching course. Terry Aldridge can keep things going while I'm away."

By the time Dad had got his first FA qualification he had enough people to back him in joining a local six-a-side league. All the original players had stayed and we were joined by three new regulars, Sonny, Ben and Alan. We had enough for a regular Under-10s team with substitutes *and* replacements.

We knew we were in business the day we turned up for training and Ben Whiting's dad proudly announced that he had a little surprise for everyone. It was our team kit! It was in the town colours, sandy yellow and white with a black and white Spellthorpe oyster catcher in a circle on the back with its wings spread over the letters SYFC.

Dad's mouth fell open. "Now look here!" he began. You could tell he was going to say that he couldn't let Mr Whiting pay for all this.

Mr Whiting brushed aside his objection. "It's fine. It's our pleasure. Me and the missus run our clothes shop. We're only too delighted to sponsor the team."

So now we had the strip, and some proper training. We were ready to take part in our first league match.

Come the day, we played pretty well, all things considered – especially in the second half when we stuck to our positions instead of dashing about together like a flock of sheep. By now little Weeksie was in goal. What he lacked in height, he made up for in speed and sheer guts.

We pegged back the score to 5-3 at one stage but the opposition, Rocky Bay, had a lot of big lads. And talk about foulers! They tapped our heels, they barged us in the back, and one kid, the flash guy they called Slick, kept using his hands and getting away with it. He was the one who took a dive to get a penalty and then scored from the spot himself. His dad, the one who kept shouting that we were rubbish, bent over and waggled his bum in the air and that was the signal for Slick to put his arms round two of his mates and do a celebration bum-waggle, too.

But when Dad gave us our team-talk at the end he said. "You did well there, lads. Yes, I know they didn't play by the rules, but don't let Rocky Bay wind you up, because you know what? We'll be back."

A Spooky Encounter!

That evening I still had the hump, so I whistled up Lolly, grabbed my new football and we trotted off round the common to let off steam.

Lolly gave me some good ball-control practice – every time I put the ball at my feet, she tried to get it off me. I don't reckon even Ronaldo could shield the ball from her for long! Still, I did work out a nice little step-over that kept her at bay for some of the time.

Then she stood back and started barking at me to kick one for her to chase. I swear I only took a three-step run-up but that ball went like a rocket! It sailed right over the lane and into the **Keep Out** wood.

"After it, Loll," I said, pointing. "Fetch!"

Good thing there was no traffic. She was over that lane like a shot, and when I dashed past the warning sign after her, I could hear her pushing through the undergrowth ahead.

"Where are you, Loll?" I called as I dodged trees and jumped over trailing brambles. She gave a double-bark and then she was quiet. I stopped and tried to hold my breath and listen.

Nothing.

I tried to make out a path but there was no sign that anyone had dared to come this way for years. It seemed a bit lighter up ahead so I pushed on in. Some pigeons clattered through the branches over my head, and set my heart pounding. I stood stock-still and listened, hoping to hear Loll nearby, but everything was eerily quiet.

"Where are you, Loll?" I said almost in a whisper.

And then I heard a strange, hollow sound: KER-POOM. KER-POOM.

My heart was still racing, but I found myself drawn towards the sound. I stepped into a clearing, the sun breaking through so brightly that everything dazzled. And there it was, the ruin of the old stand! Most of the terraces had fallen in, but the wooden pillars on one side of the

structure still supported part of the roof, so that I could make out the fading remains of a sign. Long ago it must have read: "SPELLTHORPE UNITED". Now, the only letters read: SPELL UNIT.

Something furry brushed against the back of my legs. I stifled a yell and jumped back – only to find that Lolly had pressed herself against me. I reached down to give her a pat and found that the poor dog's fur was standing up as though someone had just given her an electric shock. And yet her tail was wagging. What could it mean?

I followed her gaze to the other end of the ruined stand. We weren't alone.

A tall pale figure was kicking my football against what was left of the far end wall! He had a bushy white beard and was dressed in a dark blue uniform with a cap.

KER-POOM! boomed the ball as he side-footed it against the wall. And KER-POOM again as he toe-ended the ball and sent it rocketing towards me. If I hadn't caught it, it might have knocked the wind out of me.

"Well held, matie!" yelled the stranger and Loll began to whimper, not so much in fear as in excitement. "Have you ever played in goal?"

"Never," I said. "I'm a striker." It was weird. I was pretty sure he was a ghost, but somehow I felt safe as houses.

"Are you now?" said the figure. He turned towards me and put his hands on his hips, and I could see how bow-legged he was – as well as kind of see-through. "Striker, eh? Have you got a handle?"

"Jake," I said. "Jake Treasure. And you must be …"

"Well stap me! I spent a lifetime looking for treasure!" he cried. "Let's have another borrow of your ball, Master Treasure."

I punted it back to him and he

took it easily on his broad chest. "Lovely and light, isn't she?" he breathed enthusiastically, giving it a lively side-foot against a tree-trunk and trapping it cleanly as it returned. "Hardly feel like she's made of leather at all!"

"It's not," I said. "It's a sort of plastic."

He looked puzzled. "So … I take it you play for a team?"

"Spellthorpe Youth F.C.," I said.

"What!!!" he roared. "Who brought Spellthorpe F.C. back to life?"

"My dad!" I answered.

"Did he now!"

"Yes, well … shame we just got hammered in our first game in the league," I mumbled.

"How so?"

"They were miles bigger than us and they cheated!"

The stranger laughed. "Roughed you up, did they? Don't let that worry you. Just because you're sunk, doesn't mean you can't rise to the surface again. Here's my advice, boy. Don't get nasty; get better.

In life, you have to know where your goal is, then go for it for all you're worth!"

"That's just what my dad says. He's our manager," I said.

"Does he, by gab? Then he is definitely my sort of fellow! And there's you, a striker. I once skippered a vessel o' that name. Reckon you can strike that there doorway with your marvellous football, matie?"

He was pointing to a doorway way over to my left. Before I could answer, he rolled the ball to me and I hammered it towards the space. I was bang on target, but quick as I was, he moved quicker. Somehow he covered about twenty metres in

less than a second, taking the ball
out of the air with one hand.

"Woof!" said Loll, and I agreed
with her.

"You'll do," said the man. "You're
a striker all right. Ready for one
more challenge?"

I nodded.

"See that little nest-hole in that oak tree yonder? Put the ball in there."

It was far too small a target for me to hit normally, but I felt a surge of confidence. If I'd had a tail like Lolly, I'd have wagged it! I swung my right foot and caught the ball sweetly with my laces. It rocketed away in a beauty of a curve and cannoned off the trunk of the tree right next to the hollow.

There was a horrible shriek like a spoon scraped on a tin plate – and out of the hole squirted a brightly coloured parrot!

"Bless my flutterin' soul, if the lad ain't done it!" squawked the parrot.

"Did you hear that!" I exclaimed, turning to see whether the stranger was as gobsmacked as I was.

I was wasting my breath. He had simply melted away.

"W-where's the m-man gone?" I stammered, looking all around.

"I'll do the talking for him," answered the bird. "Keep a weather eye open. I'll come sailing by again

when the tide's on the turn. Steady
as you go, matie! Ta-ta!"

And with that, the parrot
vanished.

Squawks from the Dead

All the way home I was trying to think what I would tell Mum and Dad, but as it turned out, Dad had some news of his own.

"Look at this," he said, holding up his laptop. "I've been researching Sailor Wicks." I followed Dad's pointing finger.

Spellthorpe's bushy-bearded centre forward was famous for his rolling runs. He had a way of moving in sudden zig-zag bursts like somebody on a ship in a storm, making him almost impossible to tackle. He was a player of rare ability who could control the game and score from anywhere. Always a joker, he often wore an eye-patch and he would never play a match without bringing his parrot along for support. He was always torn between two loves: soccer and the sea.

"Are you all right, Jake?" asked Dad. "You look as though you've seen a ..."

"I'm fine," I said quickly. "Just a bit hungry, that's all."

With every game we played that season, Spellthorpe Youth made small improvements.

We got fitter and more skilful, thanks to Dad's training methods.

Bit by bit, we began to move up the league table and I was well pleased to be told that I was equal-top-scorer. Mum and I noticed a big change in Dad, too. He wasn't slaving away for Mr Robinson all the time and he seemed to be enjoying life more. Some of the lads complained that he was a bit too quiet and shy during matches compared with other coaches, which was true, but as I told them, at least he didn't swear and shout insults like some of the others.

As the season passed, I almost forgot about my meeting in the wood with … what should I call him? … the stranger. Part of me thought he must have been the ghost of Sailor Wicks and the more sensible part of me thought that I must have let my imagination run away with me. But then I was woken in the middle of one Friday night by a sharp tap on my bedroom window.

Gingerly I pulled back the curtain and there in the moonlight, swinging upside down from the wisteria, was a brightly coloured parrot. "What the heck?" I mouthed and in answer it swung down like a rainbow-coloured hammer and cracked its beak once more on the glass.

Rather than let it wake the whole house, I quickly opened the window and let the creature in.

"Leaper Jones!" it squawked. "Stoney Grove!"

"Not me!" I gasped. "Who do you want?"

The parrot started chattering straight away, all about Spellthorpe F.C.'s glory days. Rocking from claw to claw, he remembered with pride how Sailor's treasure-hunting paid for tip-top facilities at the club. "And if funds started running low, then Sailor and meself weighed anchor and sailed away again to explore a wreck or two. While we were at sea, we left the club in the hands of the Chairman. He was an ex-goalie, was Mister Leaper Jones, so Sailor used to joke about him being the safest hands in management. He thought Leaper was a good mate, see?"

The bird cocked its head. "Oh and 'tis a lonely life being a skipper," he sighed, "but I did my best to be lively company for him. On and on we sailed, and just when we had given up all hope, we struck Spanish gold.

"Dear old Sailor! Always loved a laugh, he did!" the parrot chuckled. "So when we came ashore in England, he thought it would be fun to bury the treasure under some trees at Stoney Grove. He loved the idea of sending all the club directors out in their fancy suits carrying shovels with a cunning little treasure-map to show them where to dig, hee-hee! To cap it all, he shaved off his beard, disguised himself as an old tramp, hid me under his jacket and went for a drink in The Travellers Rest."

Unhappily for Sailor, the joke turned sour. He soon discovered that Leaper Jones had stolen the funds and ruined the club! He dashed

45

along to the stadium to check it out and found the place was locked up and deserted.

"He was still bitter about it until the day he drowned," said the parrot gloomily.

Then he seemed to snap out of his sadness and tapped on the window, which I took as a signal that it was time to let him out. He hopped up on to the ledge and gave me and Loll a wink. "But the tide has turned now, matie," he said.

"So clear the decks for action!"

And with that he disappeared into the darkness.

Avast, You Spellers!

Weeksie grabbed me in the playground a week before the championship playoff. "Hey! You'll never guess who we're playing in the final!" he said, pointing his thumbs down. I didn't have to guess; I knew. It was those big-loud-horrible foulers from Rocky Bay.

"We ain't got a chance," groaned Weeksie.

"Don't worry," I said. "My dad's got a plan."

Actually, we were going to need a flipping miracle. Just to make things worse, the day before the match, Dad got a letter from Mr Robinson saying that if he was not available to devote time to his work at the weekend, he would have to "let him go". Maybe other dads just go barmy and start kicking things over when they get threats like that from their bosses. Mine just went all quiet and pale as porridge.

Come the Sunday of the match, he was so low that nothing could get a smile out of him, not Mum who had come along to cheer; not even Cam's new haircut.

The Spellthorpe Youth team was gathered by the entrance-end goal at the Old Stags' ground, shivering with nerves. Wow, it looked big – and wow! – so did the opposition. They and their supporters had already started sneering at us.

"What d'you reckon, guys," said Cam seriously, running the palm of his hand over his newly cropped hair. "Do I look hard?"

"Hard as jelly," said Robbie Settle, so he and Cam had a pretend-fight and we all started cheering and mucking about.

Normally Dad would have stepped in and settled us down. When he didn't, our supporters, parents mostly, plus a few granddads, a handful of brothers and a two baby sisters in pushchairs, started to look nervous and whisper to one another behind their hands.

The whistle went. "Do your best," Dad said. That was it.

"That wasn't much of a pep-talk," I heard Sonny mutter to Ben as we gathered in the centre circle for the toss-up. I found myself face-to face with Slick, the Bum-Waggle Kid. His lips moved slowly so that I could read them. "You're doomed," they said.

First twenty minutes, you had to agree with the Rocky Bay supporters. We were rubbish. The fact was we were getting no help from the touchline. Dad had lost his tongue, our supporters were embarrassed and we totally lost our discipline. We were flapping about like a pigeons, bunching together, missing tackles, getting out of position. The worst thing was that Slick managed to bounce one in off poor Weeksie's backside! That did our team spirit no good at all.

Let's face it, we were all scared stiff. How we kept the score down to 4-0, I have no idea.

Then I heard Dad let out a yell louder than any yell he'd ever let

out in his life.
"To your
stations, you
Spellers!" he
bellowed. Loll
threw back her head
and went, "Wa-oooooo!"
We all jumped. Dad's hair,
normally a bit floppy, was sticking up
like hedgehog quills and I soon saw
why. There was a rainbow-coloured
parrot sitting on his shoulder with its
beak close to his ear!

Nickie Palmer ran back into
position, took the ball off an attacker
and looked for someone to pass it
to. "Full steam ahead!" Dad yelled,
so Nickie did just that – went round
two players and slid it to Cam.

"Hard a-starboard!" screamed Dad. "Stand by to repel boarders!"

"Do what?" shouted Cam.

"Hit it to Jake! He's on your right, you big land-lubber!" yelled Mr Aldridge.

"Starboard! Starboard!" chanted our supporters.

The ball came sweetly across so I could take it in my stride.

"Shiver their timbers!" yelled Dad.

I was miles from the goal but I let rip.

Bang! Top starboard corner! The net hissed, the cross-bar vibrated. YEAH!!!!!!!

We were unstoppable. The crowd got behind us, really into Dad's seafaring spirit. "Sail on the port beam!" called some joker as Rocky Bay's fastest player made a charging run down our left wing.

"Avast, you Spellers!" yelled everybody else. Ben had come on as sub, and he stood his ground like the Rock of Gibraltar. By now, I'd scored twice, so half the Rocky Bay team got round me when one of our side looked as if he might pass to me.

"No!" I warned, seeing Ben nick the ball and shape up to ping it my way. But Ben was too excited by robbing

one of their best players and he sent a dangerously loose ball trickling towards me – and the three opposition-lads who stood between me and him, ready to pounce.

What happened then was downright weird. I felt the pitch rise and fall under me. It was the same feeling I had once on a rough ferry crossing to the Isle of Wight. I staggered one way, then the other, cutting through the crowd of players trying to muscle me out.

"What shall we do with the drunken sailor?" sang the crowd, taken over, as I was, by the spirit of Spellthorpe's greatest forward, Ernie Wicks. I zig-zagged, I lurched. I dodged a shoulder-charge by one player, lost their Number 5 with a step-over (my Lolly-special) and when Slick slid in to try to cripple me, I skipped over his high-kicking boots like a ten-year-old George Best.

The ref waved play on. "Full steam ahead!" roared the crowd.

KAPOOM! Goal!

Ticking off for Slick. Red card. All over.

"Brilliant, Neville!" boomed Mr Aldridge as we all charged for the touchline afterwards, waving our arms in the air. He slapped Dad on

the back with his shovel of a hand.
"You really bring out the best in
these lads. 10-4! Blimey! Who would
have thought it? What a dark horse
you are, mate! You could go far in
the game if you put your mind to it.
Couldn't he, lads?"

"NOT 'ARF!" chorused
Spellthorpe Youth F.C.

Mum couldn't contain herself.
She flung her arms round the pair
of us and wouldn't stop kissing us.

It was the same with Loll. Well,
you know what I mean. Yuck!

Treasure at Stoney Grove!

Nobody else seemed to have seen the parrot that landed on Dad's shoulder, not even Mum who had been standing right next to him. Of course I wondered, not for the first time, whether I was losing my marbles. Still, when we were driving home in the car, basking in the glow of a brilliant afternoon, I had to ask Dad what it was that had suddenly perked him up during the match.

"Perked ME up!" he said, reaching out and giving me a neck-squeeze. "What about you! You played a blinder! You were magic."

"Thanks, Dad," I said. "It must have been the advice you gave us when we lost to Rocky Bay last time."

"Oh, and what was that?" he said, all pleased.

"You said: Don't get nasty; just get better. In life you have to know where your goal is and go for it for all you're worth."

"I never said that!" he protested with a laugh. "I just said we'd be back. You must have heard that from some other smart feller!"

My heart gave a bump. He was right! It wasn't him who said that, it was the ghost of Sailor Wicks! I thought I'd better change the subject, quick. "Er, have you ever heard of a town called Stoney Grove?" I asked.

"What's that got to do with anything?"

"Just wondered, that's all."

"Well no, I don't know a town by that name," said Dad, stroking his chin. "But there is a bunch of petrified trees that sometimes appears in the sand at low tide just off Dingle Point. I remember all the excitement when a TV crew came to make a film it a couple of years ago."

I felt the hairs prickle on my neck. "Can we go there now?" I said.

"Yes, go on, love," said Mum. "We'll have fish and chips or something."

When we got down on to the sand at Dingle Point, the beach was deserted. Mum held Dad's hand and asked him in a casual way if he had actually done any work for Mr Robinson that weekend. He grinned and shook his head. "Don't worry, love," he said. "Something better is bound to turn up; you said so yourself."

Well actually, it didn't just turn up; Lolly dug it up. First she went all

electric and she started
sniffing the air like
crazy – as if she'd just
smelled
the ghost
of a
parrot!

Then she got her paws in and
started digging like a meerkat.

The rest is history.

I expect you read about it in the
papers … us finding the sea-chest
full of Spanish doubloons – and the
note in a bottle that instructed the
finder to use the treasure in any
way they could "for the benefit of
Spellthorpe United F.C."

So now you know how Dad got
the money to become the owner

and chairman of the town's brand-new football club, built on the site of the old Spellthorpe F.C. grounds.

Mum runs the office, Loll's the official mascot – and guess who's the star of the Youth Academy? Well … it had to happen, didn't it!

Dad couldn't be more chuffed. He loves his job. But can you believe it? – he *still* thinks there's no such thing as ghosts!